curvy girl for the cowboy

emma bray

one

. . .

Colton

THE SUN BEATS DOWN MERCILESSLY on my weathered skin as I survey the sprawling ranch before me. Acres of parched land stretch out as far as the eye can see, dotted with listless cattle that hang their heads in the oppressive heat. My father's legacy, now a heavy burden on my shoulders alone.

I wipe the sweat from my brow with a calloused hand, the rough fabric of my worn Stetson offering little respite from the searing rays. The ranch house looms behind me, once a haven filled with laughter and life, now a hollow reminder of all that I've lost. Ma's faded curtains still hang in the windows, threads of happier memories that unravel a little more each day.

Everywhere I turn, there are signs of disrepair—broken fences, rusted machinery, a barn roof that sags under the weight of neglect. The land thirsts for attention I can scarcely afford to give. Each morning, I rise with the sun and work until my muscles scream in protest, but it's never enough. The debts pile higher, and the silence grows thicker.

As I lead my horse back to the stable, my mind drifts to thoughts of companionship, of someone to share the load. But what woman would want a life of endless toil and lonely nights? I shake my head, dismissing the notion as foolish. And yet, a small, stubborn seed of hope takes root in my heart, whispering of a different path.

Later, as I sit at the kitchen table, bathed in the dim light of a kerosene lamp, I stare at the mail-order bride advertisement, the paper worn soft from my touch. The words blur before my tired eyes, but the promise is clear—a chance for something more. My hand trembles slightly as I reach for a pen, a man drowning grasping for a lifeline.

"To hell with it," I mutter, my voice rough with disuse. I begin to write, pouring my hopes and dreams onto the page, each word a desperate prayer cast into the void.

———

Sam

The cramped apartment feels like it's closing in on me, the air thick with the weight of broken dreams. I sit on the edge of the bed, my green eyes fixed on the faded photograph in my hands. Dad's smiling face looks back at me, forever frozen in a moment of happiness we'll never share again.

Grief constricts my throat as I trace the lines of his face, remembering the warmth of his hugs, the rumble of his laughter. He was my rock, my guiding light in a world that often felt too dark. Now, I'm adrift, lost in a sea of uncertainty.

The eviction notice on the kitchen table taunts me, a harsh reminder of the cruel realities I face. With no job and no family to turn to, my options have dwindled to a desperate few. I take a shaky breath, my fingers tightening around the glossy brochure that promises a new beginning.

Mail-Order Brides: Find Your Perfect Match! the

headline proclaims in bold, enticing letters. Beneath it, pictures of smiling couples and sprawling ranches paint a picture of a life I can scarcely imagine. A life of purpose, of belonging, of love.

I hesitate, my heart torn between the comfort of the familiar and the allure of the unknown. Can I really leave everything I've ever known behind? Can I trust a stranger to be my anchor in the storm?

As if in answer, a ray of sunlight breaks through the clouded window, illuminating the brochure in a soft, golden glow. It feels like a sign, a whisper of hope in the darkness.

With trembling hands, I reach for my phone, my decision made. As the ringback tone echoes in my ear, I close my eyes and picture a different future, one where I'm no longer alone. When a warm, friendly voice answers, I take a deep breath and speak the words that will change my life forever.

"Hello, I'm calling about the mail-order bride service. My name is Samantha Davis, and I'm ready for a new start."

The voice on the other end of the line is warm and inviting, a soothing balm to my frayed nerves. "Welcome, Samantha. We're here to help you find your perfect match. Can you tell me a little about yourself and what you're looking for in a partner?"

I pause, the question catching me off guard.

What am I looking for? Stability, companionship, a chance at a better life? The words feel inadequate, but I forge ahead. "I'm looking for someone kind and hardworking, someone who values family and wants to build a life together. I'm not afraid of hard work, and I'm ready for a fresh start."

There's a gentle hum of understanding from the other end. "I think we may have just the match for you. His name is Colton Westbrook, and he owns a ranch in Montana. He's a bit older, but he's a good man looking for a partner to share his life with. Would you like me to send you his profile?"

My heart skips a beat at the mention of Montana, a world away from the suffocating familiarity of my hometown. "Yes, please," I manage, my voice barely above a whisper.

Moments later, my phone chimes with an incoming message. I open it with shaking hands, and Colton's rugged face fills the screen. His piercing blue eyes seem to stare straight into my soul, and I feel a flutter of something I can't quite name.

As I read through his profile, I'm struck by the honesty in his words. He doesn't try to paint himself as perfect, but rather as a man who's faced his share of struggles and is looking for someone to weather the storms with him.

Before I can second-guess myself, I find my fingers flying across the screen, crafting a message to this man who feels like a lifeline in a sea of uncertainty.

"Hello, Colton. I'm Samantha, but everyone calls me Sam. I saw your profile and felt a connection. I know we're strangers, but I'm willing to take a chance if you are. Life has dealt us both some hard blows, but maybe together, we can find a way to heal."

I hit send before I lose my nerve, my heart pounding in my chest. As I wait for his response, I can't help but wonder if I've officially gone nuts.

But, honestly? What do I have to lose?

two

. . .

Sam

THE SPRAWLING RANCH stretches out before me, an endless sea of green pastures and rolling hills under the vast blue Montana sky. My heart races as the pickup truck rumbles up the long dirt driveway, kicking up clouds of dust. This is it—my new home, my new life. As a bride to a man I barely know.

The truck lurches to a stop and the door opens. Colton Westbrook stands on the other side, his tall, broad frame filling the doorway. My breath catches. He's even more rugged and handsome than his photo—all chiseled features, sun-bronzed skin, and piercing blue eyes that seem to see right through me. I feel his gaze rake over my curvy figure as I climb out of the truck, suddenly self-conscious in my yellow sundress.

"You must be Samantha," he says, his deep, gravelly voice sending shivers down my spine. "Welcome to Westbrook Ranch."

"It's Sam," I manage with a shy smile, tucking a stray auburn curl behind my ear. "Thank you. It's beautiful here."

He nods curtly and grabs my suitcase, his arm muscles flexing under his white button-down shirt. I follow him up the porch steps to the sprawling farmhouse, my legs trembling slightly, though from nerves or anticipation I can't tell. The man is built like a mountain—solid, strong, immovable. And he's my husband now. The thought both thrills and terrifies me.

As we step inside, the rich scent of leather and pine envelops me. It feels like home already, cozy and inviting. But the silent tension crackling between Colton and me fills the air with a strange energy.

I glance up and find his blue eyes fixed on me again, swirling with some unreadable emotion. Desire? Regret? I look away quickly, my cheeks flushing hot. What have I gotten myself into? Can I really do this—be a wife to this quiet, intimidating cowboy?

I take a deep breath, willing myself to be brave, to have hope. This is my chance for a new beginning, for love and family and belonging.

I just pray I'm strong enough to grab it.

———

Colton

"Let me show you around." I tear my gaze away from Samantha's soft curves and lead her through the house, my pulse beating faster than a spooked stallion. Lord Almighty, she's a vision. When she stepped out of that truck in her little yellow dress, mile-long legs stretched out, red curls tumbling down her back, I could barely breathe. I almost regret this whole mail order bride scheme. How am I supposed to focus on the ranch with her around as a distraction?

"The barns are out this way." I guide her out the back door, struggling to keep my eyes ahead as she follows behind me. Her bright green eyes are too damn inviting, drawing me in like quicksand. I have to keep my distance if this is going to work. I have a ranch to save and no time for romance.

"Do you have many horses?" Her musical voice breaks the tense silence as we enter the stables. I nod and point out the stalls.

"'Bout twenty right now. Used to be more, before..." I let my words trail off, unwilling to unpack the grief still looming over this ranch like a dark cloud.

Sam just smiles softly. "They're beautiful. I've always loved horses." She reaches out to stroke a white mare's nose and I'm mesmerized by her gentleness, her natural ease around the animals.

Dragging my eyes away, I clear my throat and head out of the stable. "I'll show you the rest."

We walk along the fences and I point out the different pastures and equipment, hyper aware of her presence beside me, the way the sun illuminates the hints of red in her hair, the sweet floral scent that wafts my way when she turns her head. It's unnerving. I'm used to hard work, sweat and dirt, the simple routines of ranch life. I don't know what the hell to do with a woman like Samantha. Especially one I have to call my wife.

One who's way too pretty for a thirty-five-year-old man like me. There's no way I could ever be good enough for her. I don't know what situation caused her to sign up for a mail-order bride service, but I know she has to be desperate to agree to something like this.

What I can't figure is how is a pretty thing like this not already married to some young buck? Why did she agree to marry some stranger like me?

I can only pray this marriage of convenience doesn't unravel everything I've been working for. And that I can keep my growing desire for this captivating woman locked down deep, where it can't burn us both to cinders.

———

Sam

The scrape of forks against plates echoes uncomfortably loud in the stillness of the dining room. I sneak a glance at Colton, his eyes fixed intently on his meal as if the mashed potatoes might reveal the secrets of the universe. The air feels thick, weighted with all the words we're not saying.

I clear my throat. "This is delicious. Did you make it yourself?"

Colton grunts, sparing me the briefest of glances. "Mhm. Not much of a cook but I get by." He shovels another forkful into his mouth.

"Well, I'd be happy to help out in the kitchen. It's the least I can do." I aim for lightness but it falls flat in the oppressive quiet.

His eyes flicker to mine, stormy blue depths unreadable. "You don't need to do that. I didn't bring you here to be my maid."

I flush, stung by his dismissiveness. "I know that. I just...I want to contribute somehow. Earn my keep."

Colton sets down his fork with a sigh. "You're not a burden, Samantha." His voice gentles a fraction. "I wouldn't have agreed to this arrangement if I didn't think it would be mutually beneficial."

"Beneficial. Right." The words feel brittle on my tongue. Is that all I am to him? A business transaction?

I mean, I of course I am. I guess. Right? I have no right to be offended. Hell, I don't know.

Silence descends once more as we finish our meal. I can't shake the gnawing fear that he regrets this already, regrets *me*. That I've left everything behind for an illusion of belonging.

My face colors. Oh my god. What if I'm too curvy for him? I know curves as thick as mine aren't every man's cup of tea. What if I'm not pretty enough?

I touch my hair self-consciously. What if he hates redheads?

All the what-ifs are still spinning through my mind when Colton stands abruptly, chair scraping harshly against the floor. I nearly jump out of my skin. "I have some things to take care of. I'll clean up later," he says gruffly.

He's gone before I can formulate a response, his heavy footsteps echoing in the hallway. I slump back in my seat, appetite evaporated. Is this what our life together will be? Ships passing in the night, never quite connecting?

I can only hope that time will thaw the icy reserve of my new husband. And pray that I haven't made a terrible mistake.

———

Colton

I stride down the hall, blood pounding in my ears, a roaring that drowns out everything but the need clawing under my skin. The need to touch her. To taste her. To bury myself in her softness and never come up for air.

Damn it all to hell.

I slam into my bedroom, locking the door behind me. My cock is harder than railroad iron, jutting against the confines of my jeans. All through that torturous meal, I couldn't stop imagining spreading Samantha out on the table, hiking that skirt up her creamy thighs, feasting on her sweet nectar until she begged for mercy.

The shame of it twists like a knife in my gut. She's not a object for me to rut against. She's my wife. A wife I barely know but who deserves more respect than the filthy fantasies running through my head.

I lean my forehead against the door, trying to catch my breath. To will the raging lust away. But it's no use. Growling in frustration, I yank open my fly, wrapping a rough hand around my aching erection. I pump furiously, images of Samantha's plush lips, the elegant curve of her neck, her full breasts creating a tormenting slideshow in my mind.

It doesn't take long. Half a dozen strokes and I'm coming hard, painting my fist and the door with ropey white streams. I muffle my groan into my shoulder, knees nearly buckling from the force of my release.

As the haze of pleasure fades, the disgust rushes in. What kind of man am I, objectifying my own wife? Treating her like a means to an end?

I clean myself off methodically, regret a lead weight in my stomach. This can't happen again. I won't let it. Samantha deserves a real husband, not a lecherous fool who can't keep it in his pants.

I'll be better.

I have to be.

For her.

three

. . .

Sam

THE GENTLE SWAY of the clothesline draws my eye as I pin up freshly laundered shirts, their worn cotton soft beneath my fingers. A warm breeze carries the scent of sun-warmed leather and horses, the symphony of ranch life playing in the distance—hooves clopping, cattle lowing, the creak of a saddle.

I feel his gaze before I see him. A tingle goes down my spine.

Colton.

He's by the barn, those piercing blue eyes watching me from under the brim of his hat before he turns away, shoulders straight as an arrow as he strides towards the corrals. The air feels charged when he's near, like the heavy stillness before a thunderstorm.

Sighing, I gather the empty laundry basket and head inside the rustic ranch house that still doesn't quite feel like home. In the kitchen, late afternoon light slants in, illuminating the yellow gingham curtains. I start preparing supper, the simple rituals of chopping vegetables and kneading dough grounding me.

It's clear that my role here is to tend to the house while he does all the hard work outside.

Where we are completely separate.

I sigh and go about my tasks, and my mind inevitably wanders to Dad.

Lost in thought, a tear slips down my cheek before I even realize I'm crying. Memories of cooking with Dad flood my mind—his booming laugh, strong hands guiding mine, the way he'd sneak bites when he thought I wasn't looking. God I miss him, an ache so deep in my chest I can hardly breathe.

The creak of a floorboard startles me, and I turn to find Colton frozen in the doorway, hat in hand, an unreadable expression on his rugged face. "You alright there darlin'?" His deep gravelly drawl sends a shiver through me.

Hastily, I wipe at my cheeks. "I'm fine, I just...I recently lost my dad..." My voice cracks and I swallow hard.

Two strides and he's in front of me, calloused thumb tentatively brushing away a tear. "It's okay, I understand." His blue eyes are soft, almost tender. "Grief has a way of sneaking up on you."

I nod, not trusting myself to speak. Slowly, giving me time to pull away, he folds me into his strong arms. I stiffen for a heartbeat before melting into his solid warmth, breathing in the scent of him —leather, horses, and something uniquely Colton.

"When I lost my Pa, felt like the ground dropped out from under me. Still does some days." His deep rumble vibrates through me where my cheek presses to his chest. My arms tighten around his waist. "You're not alone Sam. I'm here."

Hope blooms fragile and bright in my chest, his quiet words wrapping around my bruised heart like a balm. Maybe, just maybe, I've found a safe harbor after the storms. In the shelter of Colton's embrace, for the first time since Dad died, I feel the tiniest spark of something that might be home.

A shuddering breath escapes me as I cling to Colton, this man who is still a stranger yet feels like a lifeline in the tempest of my grief. His hand rubs soothing circles on my back, calluses catching on the worn fabric of my dress. Time seems to still, narrowing down to the two of us, the golden late-day light, the hush of our mingled breathing.

Slowly, reluctantly, I lift my head from the solid strength of his chest, my eyes finding his. The blue depths hold understanding, empathy, and a flicker of something heated that sends a flush crawling up my neck. Awareness prickles over my skin, the air suddenly thick, charged with a tension I can't name.

Colton's gaze drops to my mouth, his own parting slightly. Rough thumbs brush my cheek-bones, tilting my face up to his. I feel the ghost of his breath on my lips, the rasp of his stubble. My pulse kicks into a gallop. The look on his face…I don't know what it means, but it has me tied all up in knots.

His scent intoxicates me—leather, sweat, and something wild and untamed that speaks to a primal part of me. The rough pads of his thumbs caress my tear-stained cheeks with a gentleness that belies their strength. I'm drowning in the fath-omless blue of his eyes, falling into their stormy depths.

Time stretches taut between us, the very air seeming to hold its breath. Colton's callused palm slides to the nape of my neck, his touch igniting sparks beneath my skin. He leans in, his lips so close to mine.

Oh my god. He's going to kiss me.

I let out a shaky breath, and then as quickly as it almost happened, it stops.

Colton releases me, takes off his hat and runs a hand through his hair, ruffling it as he looks down, mumbles something about having to get back to work and turns swiftly on his heel and leaves.

Only when he's gone do I realize I'm trembling, though with what I don't know.

four

. . .

Colton

THE SUN'S just cresting over the horizon when I spot Sam striding across the ranch yard, her auburn hair glinting in the early morning light. She's wearing faded jeans that hug her curves and a plaid shirt with the sleeves rolled up, ready for work. It catches me off guard.

"Mornin' darlin'," I call out, trying to hide my surprise. "You're up awful early."

She flashes me a smile that makes something stir deep in my chest. "Thought I'd lend a hand with the chores today. If that's alright with you?"

I hesitate, not wanting to burden her with the hard labor of ranch life. But there's a determined gleam in her green eyes that tells me she won't take no for an answer. And isn't that part of why I got a wife? For help? Still, I want to baby her and don't want her working herself too hard. Not that I don't think she can handle it. Just I have this innate urge to take care of her.

Because in my mind, she's *mine*.

"Alright then," I concede, tipping my hat. "Reckon I could use the help."

We set to work, side by side, the silence broken only by the lowing of cattle and the creak of leather. I steal glances at her as she hefts hay bales, admiring the sheen of sweat on her brow and the strength in her arms. She meets my gaze and I quickly look away, feeling like a schoolboy caught staring.

As the day wears on, we find ourselves in the corrals, wrangling calves for branding. I watch as Sam picks up a lasso, a look of concentration on her face as she tries to rope a particularly feisty calf. She swings and misses, the rope falling short.

"Here, let me show you," I offer, coming up behind her. I cover her hands with mine, feeling the softness of her skin, breathing in the sweet scent of her hair. Together we swing the lasso, letting it fly. It lands true, catching the calf around the neck.

"I did it!" she exclaims, turning to face me, her eyes shining with pride.

Suddenly I'm acutely aware of how close we are, our bodies nearly touching. I feel a rush of heat that has nothing to do with the Texas sun. She must feel it too because her breath catches and her cheeks flush pink.

For a moment we just stare at each other, something unspoken passing between us. I'm seized by the sudden urge to kiss her, to taste those soft, full lips. But I resist, stepping back and clearing my throat.

"Good job," I manage to say, my voice coming out rougher than I intend.

The moment stretches between us, taut and electric, before Sam breaks the tension with a laugh. "Guess I'm a natural," she jokes, but there's a breathless quality to her voice that sends a shiver down my spine.

We return to work, but the air feels charged now, heavy with unspoken desire. Every brush of her hand against mine as we work side by side feels like a jolt of lightning. I find myself watching her more and more, entranced by the sway of her hips, the curve of her neck, the fullness of her lips.

She catches me staring and holds my gaze, her eyes smoldering with an intensity that makes my blood run hot. I swallow hard, trying to rein in the desire that's raging through me. But it's like trying to stop a wildfire with a bucket of water.

As the sun starts to dip towards the horizon, we finish up the last of the chores. Sam stretches, her shirt riding up to reveal a strip of creamy skin. I quickly avert my eyes, busying myself with coiling up a length of rope.

"I'm gonna head in and start on supper," she says, her voice soft and inviting. "Care to join me?"

I hesitate, torn between the need to keep my distance and the overwhelming desire to be near her. But the thought of sharing a meal with her, of sitting across the table and watching the candle-light dance in her eyes, is too tempting to resist.

"I'd like that," I reply, my voice coming out low and husky.

We walk back to the house together, our arms brushing with each step. The tension between us is palpable, like a string pulled taut, ready to snap at any moment.

Inside, Sam sets to work in the kitchen, humming softly to herself as she chops vegetables and stirs pots. I lean against the doorframe, watching her, marveling at the way she's brought life and warmth back into this old house.

She looks up, catching me in her gaze, and smiles. "Supper's almost ready. Why don't you go wash up?"

I nod, reluctant to leave her even for a moment. But I force myself to go, splashing cool water on my face and trying to calm the pounding of my heart.

When I return, the table is set with a simple but hearty meal. Sam's face is flushed from the heat of the stove, tendrils of hair escaping from her braid. She looks utterly beautiful.

We sit down to eat, the silence broken only by the clink of cutlery and the occasional murmured compliment about the food. But under the table, our knees brush, sending sparks of electricity through me.

"This is delicious," I tell her, meaning every word. "You're a mighty fine cook, darlin'."

She ducks her head, pleased and a little embarrassed by the praise. "I'm glad you like it."

We finish eating and I insist on helping her clean up, our hands bumping and grazing as we wash and dry the dishes. Every touch feels like a brand, searing into my skin.

Finally, the kitchen is clean and there's nothing left to do but say goodnight. We linger in the doorway, neither of us ready to part.

"Thank you for today," Sam says softly, her eyes searching mine. "I enjoyed working with you."

"I enjoyed it too," I admit, my voice rough with emotion. "But I should be the one thankin' you. You were a mighty big help." My brow furrows as I rush to add, "but I don't want you taxing yourself every day. You got enough to do in here. I can handle the outdoors."

Sam tilts her head, a playful smile tugging at her lips. "You don't think I can handle it, Cowboy?"

Her teasing tone sends a rush of heat through me. I step closer, drawn to her like a moth to a flame. "I know you can handle it. You're the toughest woman I've ever met. But I also know you've got a heart as big as Texas, and you'll work yourself to the bone if I let you."

She laughs softly, the sound wrapping around me like a warm breeze. "You're not wrong. But I want to help, Colton. I want to be your partner."

I know she didn't mean it the way my brain takes it, but the implication in her words makes my heart hammer against my ribs. I reach out, cupping her cheek in my calloused palm. Her skin is soft as silk, and I can feel her pulse fluttering beneath my fingertips.

"Sam," I breathe, my voice rough with longing. "You are my partner. But you're also my wife. And I aim to take care of you, like a husband should."

Her eyes darken, the green turning to smoky emerald. "I can take care of you too."

A groan rumbles in my chest. This beautiful, sweet thing is killing me. I've never wanted anyone the way I want her, with a need that goes soul-deep. "Darlin', you're doing just fine," I tell her, my thumb stroking the delicate line of her jaw.

Damn it all to hell, I've got to stop touching her, or I won't be able to control myself.

One look into her eyes, and it's clear she's innocent as hell. She has no idea what she's doing to me or the filthy thoughts running through my head right now.

I finally muster up the strength to take a step back from her. "Go on and rest. You've more than earned it. I'll take care of the clean-up here."

She opens her mouth as if she's going to speak before she closes it and nods. "Okay."

She might not want to admit it, but I see the weariness in her eyes. Today wore her out. She's not used to that kind of work. Hell, that kind of work wears the most seasoned cowboy out.

"Goodnight, Colton," she tells me before she turns to head to her bedroom.

My throat is so tight as I watch her hips sway as she walks away from me, I can barely respond, "Goodnight, darlin'."

My perfect yet untouchable wife.

five

. . .

Colton

THE SUN HANGS low over the dusty horizon as I watch her from across the corral, the fading light catching in her auburn waves. Sam's reaching up to brush a horse's muzzle, murmuring gentle words I can't quite make out. Even from this distance, her beauty steals my breath. Those soft curves, that radiant smile, those eyes that shimmer like emeralds—she's a vision in a simple blue dress and boots.

I swallow hard past the lump in my throat. What business do I have thinking' on her like this?

I'm supposed to be protecting' her, not undressing' her with my eyes. She deserves a better man than a rough-hewn cowboy barely keeping' his ranch from foreclosure. A girl like that...she'd never truly want the likes of me.

Abruptly, I turn away before she catches me staring'. Distance. That's what I need. Some space between us 'fore I do something' mighty stupid, like pull her into my arms and...

No. I shake my head, tryin' to clear it. Can't be thinking' like that. I busy myself with the saddle I'm mending', forcing my eyes down, jaw clenched tight enough to ache.

"Colton?" Her sweet voice drifts over, making' my heart thump harder against my ribs. "You've been awful quiet today. Everything alright?"

"Fine," I manage to grunt, not lookin' up. "Just got a lot of work to do, is all."

Silence stretches between us, thick with unsaid things. I risk a glance her way. Hurt flickers across her delicate features before she masks it with a tight smile.

"Of course. I'll just...leave you to it then." Her voice wavers slightly before she turns to walk away, skirts swishing around her ankles.

Guilt twists in my gut as I watch her go, shoulders slumped, arms wrapped around herself. I'm hurting her with my distance, I know it. Confusing her. But it's for the best. She'll realize soon enough she made a mistake coming here, thinking a mail-order marriage was the answer.

She deserves happiness, love, a future. And I...I can't give her any of that. No matter how badly I ache to.

———

The chill of the night air seeps into my bones as I stare out the kitchen window, watching moonlight paint the ranch in shades of silver and shadow. Sleep won't come, not with her sleeping under my roof, just down the hall.

I'm a damned fool. What was I thinking, bringing her here? A young, beautiful woman, alone on a sprawling ranch with a man near old enough to be her daddy. People will talk. I don't give two fucks what they think of me.

But *her*.

My chest aches at the thought of anyone saying anything bad about her. She's the most perfect angel in this world. She doesn't deserve that shame.

A creak of a floorboard makes me tense, hand tightening on my coffee mug. I turn to see Sam standing' in the doorway, wrapped in a quilt, hair tousled from her pillow. Even sleep-rumpled, she steals my breath.

"Couldn't sleep either?" She ventures softly, green eyes glimmering' in the low light.

I clear my throat, lookin' away. "Suppose not."

She pads closer on bare feet. "Colton, have I...have I done something to upset you?" Her voice trembles, making' my chest ache. "You've barely spoken to me in days. If you're regretting this arrangement, I can-"

"No," I cut her off gruffly, the thought of her leaving' panicking' me more than it should. "You ain't done nothin' wrong. It's not...it's me, alright?"

Her brow furrows. "I don't understand."

I exhale hard, rubbing a hand over my stubbled jaw. How can I make her see? Make her understand the battle raging' inside me?

"If you would just talk to me—" she begins.

"Dammit, Sam, I'm tryin' to protect you!" I slam my mug down, coffee sloshing over the rim. "Can't you see that?"

She flinches but doesn't back down, chin lifted, meet in' my glare head on. "I don't need your protection. I need you to be honest with me. To talk to me. Let me in, Colton. Please."

The plea in her voice undoes me. I feel myself cracking', defenses fallen'. Lord help me, but I want to. I want nothin' more than to let her in, to keep her, cherish her, love her like she deserves.

But I can't. If I ever take this curvy thing in my arms, it's going to be no holds barred. I'll turn into a fucking beast. I'll rip her virginity to shreds. I'm assuming she's a virgin because the thought of another man ever taking her drives me insane with jealousy. I can't bear the thought of it.

And thinking of her pussy has me hard as steel and aching again.

"I think...I think you should go back to bed," I rasp, throat raw with pent up emotions. "We got an early mornin' tomorrow."

Her eyes swim with tears she refuses to let fall. "Is that really what you want? For me to go?"

I can't face her. Can't watch her cry knowing' I'm the cause. "It's for the best."

A shuddering breath escapes her. Then she's turning, fleeing the kitchen, the slamming of her bedroom door echoing through the silent house like a gunshot.

I slump back against the counter, head bowed, heart shattered. What have I done?

———

I sit in the kitchen for a long time, miserable at the thought of hurting Sam before the creak of the screen door snaps me out of my misery. I'm moving' before I can think better of it, long strides eating up the distance to the porch. "Sam, wait!"

She's halfway down the steps, arms wrapped tight around herself like she's holding' herself together. The sight of her—so small, so broken—tears me apart.

"Leave me alone, Colton," she throws over her shoulder, voice thick with tears.

I catch her arm, spinning her to face me. "I can't."

"Why?" she demands, green eyes flashing with a mix of anger and confusion. "You've made it perfectly clear you don't want me here."

"That's not true." The words come out low and fierce, surprising us both with their intensity.

She searches my face, lookin' for the lie. "Then what is it? Because I don't understand. One minute you're kind to me, treating me like I matter, and the next you're pushing me away."

I cup her face, thumbs brushing away the tears she couldn't hold back any longer. "You do matter, darlin'. More than you know."

"Then why-"

I bring my lips close to hers.

So close. So fucking close. I'm dying to taste her.

But I somehow muster up every ounce of restraint I have and rasp, "Go back to bed. We're both tired and cranky after a long day."

She looks like she might argue, but maybe she sees the tension in my body, the way my arms are trembling with the effort it takes me to keep from ravishing her right here and now.

She swallows and turns to obey wordlessly.

As soon as I hear her door shut, I growl in frustration and pull my aching cock from my pants, beating it furiously like a crazed animal.

———

Sam

I lean against my closed bedroom door, heart pounding, mind reeling. What just happened out there? The way Colton looked at me, touched me...I felt it down to my very soul. The heat, the longing, the desire barely restrained.

But why? Why pull me close only to push me away again? I don't understand him. One moment he's gazing at me like I'm the only woman in the world, the next he's shutting me out cold.

Frustrated tears burn my eyes as I slump down to the floor, hugging my knees to my chest. Is it me? Is there something wrong with me that he finds so repulsive?

I thought...I thought we had a connection. That maybe, just maybe, he could come to care for me the way I'm starting to care for him, despite my best intentions.

But apparently I'm a fool. A naive little girl with her head in the clouds, chasing dreams that will never come true.

Shame and embarrassment choke me. I never should have come here. Never should have signed up for that ridiculous mail-order bride service. What was I thinking?

That a rough, rugged cowboy like Colton could ever truly want a soft, inexperienced thing like me? I press my face into my hands, shoulders shaking with silent sobs.

I should leave. First thing in the morning, I should pack my meager belongings and go. Spare us both any further humiliation. He's made it clear he doesn't want me here, doesn't want *me*. Staying will only lead to more heartache.

But where would I go? I have nothing and no

one to return to. This ranch, this marriage...it was my last hope. Without it, I'm lost. Adrift.

Alone.

The thought sends a fresh wave of despair crashing over me. I curl into myself tighter, trying to hold the broken pieces of my heart together.

six

. . .

Sam

THE MORNING SUN casts long shadows across the ranch as I make my way to the stables, my boots crunching on the gravel path. A gentle breeze carries the scent of hay and leather, mingling with the earthy aroma of the horses. I focus on the tasks at hand, determined to keep my mind off Colton and the confusing emotions swirling within me.

As I brush down Midnight, Colton's favorite mare, I hear footsteps approaching. My heart quickens, knowing it's him before I even turn around. I keep my eyes on the horse, my hands moving in rhythmic strokes.

"Mornin' Sam," Colton says, his deep voice sending a shiver down my spine. "You're up early."

I nod, not trusting myself to speak. His presence is overwhelming, filling the stable with a tension that's both thrilling and terrifying. I can feel his gaze on me, intense and unwavering.

Colton moves closer, reaching out to stroke Midnight's muzzle. His hand brushes against mine, and I jerk away as if burned. He frowns, his blue eyes clouding with confusion and hurt.

"Sam, I..." He starts, then falters. "I'm sorry for pushin' you away. It's not what I want, but I'm scared of lettin' you down."

I turn to face him, my heart hammering in my chest. His rugged features are softened by vulnerability, and I ache to reach out and comfort him. But I keep my arms at my sides, my guard firmly in place.

"I understand, Colton," I say softly. "You have a lot on your plate. I don't want to be a burden."

He shakes his head vehemently. "You could never be a burden, darlin'. The truth is, I'm...I'm fallin' for you, hard and fast. And it terrifies me. Because I don't think you understand...I'm fucking obsessed with you. If we ever become man and wife in every sense of the word, I won't be able to control myself. You'll be mine. Do you understand what I'm saying to you, honey?"

My breath catches in my throat, his words hanging in the air between us. The admission is both exhilarating and daunting, a promise of something beautiful and dangerous.

Colton takes a step closer, his hand cupping my cheek. His touch is rough and gentle all at once, igniting a fire within me that threatens to consume us both.

"I want to be with you, Sam," he whispers, his breath hot against my skin. "But I need to know if you feel the same. Heaven knows I ain't ever gonna be good enough for you. A washed-up old cowboy like me. And I feel like I'm a selfish asshole for even expecting a beautiful thing like you to tie yourself to me, but fuck, I want you to."

I frown at his words. He acts like he's eighty. He's only thirty-five, and I'm twenty. He's not *that* much older than me.

Colton clears his throat and speaks roughly, "The ball's in your court now, honey."

I stare into his eyes, searching for the truth behind his words. The intensity of his gaze is overwhelming, a silent plea for understanding and acceptance.

The dying sunlight paints the ranch in ethereal

shades of gold and orange as I stand before Colton, my heart beating an unsteady rhythm. His rugged features soften, those piercing blue eyes capturing mine with an intensity that both thrills and terrifies me.

"Colton, I..." My voice wavers, the words catching in my throat. "It's just hard for me to believe that someone like you could want someone like me."

His brows furrow, a hint of confusion clouding his gaze. "What do you mean?"

I avert my eyes, suddenly finding the worn floorboards beneath my feet utterly fascinating. "Look at me. I'm not exactly the type of woman men like you usually go for." My hands nervously smooth over my curves, accentuating the very insecurities that plague my thoughts.

Colton steps closer, the heat of his body enveloping me like a comforting blanket. His calloused fingers gently tilt my chin upward, forcing me to meet his unwavering gaze. "Sam, honey, you're everything I didn't know I needed. Hell, it's taken every ounce of my self-control to not ravish you every time I see you. You've given me a permanent case of blue balls. I've been beating off every night thinking of you, torturing myself knowing your sweet self was just down the hallway."

My mouth falls open in show, but before I can respond, his lips descend upon mine, capturing them in a searing kiss that steals the breath from my lungs. His strong arms encircle my waist, pulling me flush against his muscular frame. I melt into his embrace, my hands instinctively clutching at his broad shoulders for support.

As the kiss deepens, Colton's hips begin to move, grinding against me through the layers of our clothing, letting me feel in no uncertain terms what I do to him.

A ragged groan escapes his throat, vibrating against my lips. He breaks the kiss, his breath hot against my skin as he rasps, "You crazy girl, do you see what you do to me? Not want you? Honey, I *burn* for you."

My heart soars at his words, a heady mix of desire and disbelief coursing through my veins. Could it be true? Could this rugged, handsome cowboy truly want *me*, curves and all? The evidence of his arousal pressing insistently against my hip suggests that yes, indeed, he does.

My fingers tremble as I hesitantly explore the planes of Colton's chest, the heat of his skin seeping through the worn fabric of his shirt. The air between us crackles with tension, the silence broken only by the soft rustling of clothing and the pounding of my own heart.

Colton's hands slide lower, his touch setting my nerves alight as he cups my curves possessively. "Every inch of you belongs to me now, darlin'," he murmurs, his voice a low rumble that sends shivers down my spine.

I gaze up at him through my lashes, feeling both vulnerable and powerful under the intensity of his stare. "Show me," I whisper, surprised by my own boldness. "Make me yours."

A growl emanates from deep within Colton's chest as he lifts me effortlessly, carrying me towards the bedroom with long, purposeful strides. He lays me down on the soft quilt, his body covering mine like a protective shield.

Clothes are shed with fumbling urgency, barriers discarded until nothing remains between us but heated skin and shared breaths. Colton's hands map the contours of my body, his touch reverent yet demanding, igniting a fire in my veins.

"Look at you, all these beautiful curves. You drive me insane, darlin'," Colton groans as he strokes his cock while he gazes down at me.

I can't stop staring at him—the immense length and girth of him. I bite my lip, worry taking over.

How in the hell is he going to fit *that* inside me?

Colton picks up on my worry becuase he suddenly stops, his brow furrowing. "What's wrong, honey?"

My cheeks flush as I admit, "It's just...I've never done this before, and you seem so..."I gesture toward his cock before I finish lamely,"big."

Colton's eyes widen, relief and tenderness mingling in their depths. "Never?" he asks softly, his hand reaching out to gently caress my cheek.

I shake my head, feeling a wave of vulnerability wash over me. "No. I...I've never had a boyfriend. And then my father died, and I was just trying to survive..." My voice trails off, the weight of my past hanging heavy in the air.

Colton's expression softens, understanding dawning on his rugged features. "Oh, darlin'," he murmurs, his thumb brushing away a stray tear that I hadn't even realized had escaped. "We'll take it slow, I promise. I'll make it so good for you."

His words, spoken with such sincerity and care, melt away the last of my reservations. I nod, trusting him completely as I whisper, "I want you, Colton. All of you."

A shudder runs through his muscular frame at my declaration. He lowers his head, his lips trailing feather-light kisses along the column of my neck, his beard rasping deliciously against my sensitive skin. "Good, honey, because I want every inch of you. You're going to be mine. All mine. You understand that, honey?"

I swallow and nod, warmth washing over me at his possessiveness. It makes me feel *wanted*. I want to belong to him.

"Then, you just lay there and let me take care of you, darlin'," he says before he drops to his knees and pulls me to the edge of the bed.

I gasp when I see his head between my thighs, and then I feel his tongue lick me down *there*.

A strangled cry escapes my lips as Colton's tongue delves into my most intimate folds, exploring, teasing, igniting a firestorm of sensation that threatens to consume me whole. My hands fist in the quilt beneath me, my hips arching instinctively against his mouth, seeking more of that exquisite pleasure.

Colton groans, the sound vibrating through my core as he laps at my slick heat with increasing fervor. His hands grip my thighs, spreading me wider, opening me fully to his sensual onslaught. Each stroke of his tongue sends bolts of lightning racing through my veins, coiling tighter and tighter in my lower belly.

"Oh, God, Colton," I whimper, my head thrashing against the pillows as he focuses his attention on the sensitive bundle of nerves at the apex of my thighs. He suckles me gently, the scrape of his beard against my tender flesh only heightening the intensity of the sensation.

My thighs begin to tremble, my body wound tighter than a bowstring as he drives me closer and closer to the edge of something I've never known before. "Please," I beg, scarcely recognizing my own voice, breathy and desperate with need.

Colton redoubles his efforts, one hand sliding up to cup my breast, his thumb grazing over my pebbled nipple in tandem with the strokes of his tongue. It's too much, the dual sensations overwhelming me, pushing me over the precipice into a chasm of blinding ecstasy.

I shatter beneath him, my world fragmenting into a kaleidoscope of colors and sensations as wave after wave of pleasure crashes over me. Colton gentles me through it, his touch turning soothing as he coaxes out every last tremor until I'm left boneless and sated beneath him.

He crawls up my body, his eyes glittering with masculine pride and undisguised hunger as he settles between my thighs. I can feel the hot, hard length of him pressing against my entrance, and a frisson of nervousness flutters through me despite the languid afterglow.

"I've got you, darlin'," Colton murmurs, sensing my apprehension. He brushes a tender kiss against my lips, the taste of my own essence lingering on his tongue. "Just relax and let me make you feel good."

With infinite care, he begins to push forward, the blunt head of his cock breaching my virgin entrance inch by excruciating inch. There's a moment of resistance, a sharp pinch of pain that has me stiffening beneath him, but Colton soothes me with whispered endearments and gentle caresses until I relax once more.

"That's it, honey. Take all of me," he groans as he hilts himself fully inside me, stretching me, filling me in a way I've never known before. It's an exquisite ache, a delicious fullness that has me arching against him, my body instinctively seeking more.

Colton stills above me, his breath coming in ragged pants as he fights for control. I can feel the tension thrumming through his muscular frame, the barely leashed power simmering just beneath the surface. His gaze locks with mine, those piercing blue eyes dark with desire and something deeper, something that steals the breath from my lungs.

"You feel so damn good, darlin'," he rasps, his

voice rough with emotion. "So tight and perfect, like you were made just for me."

His words send a thrill racing down my spine, igniting a fire in my veins that threatens to consume me whole. I lift my hips experimentally, reveling in the drag of his thick length inside me, the way he stretches me so exquisitely.

Colton groans, his fingers digging into the soft flesh of my hips as he begins to move, slow and deep, each thrust stoking the embers of my desire higher and higher. The room fills with the sounds of our lovemaking, the creak of the bed mingling with our ragged breaths and soft moans.

I lose myself in the sensations, in the slide of his sweat-slicked skin against mine, the delicious friction of his body moving inside me. The world narrows down to this moment, to the exquisite pleasure building between us, coiling tighter and tighter with each thrust.

Colton's pace quickens, his control slipping as he chases his own release. His hand slips between our bodies, finding the sensitive bundle of nerves at the apex of my thighs, stroking me in time with his increasingly erratic thrusts.

"Come for me, Sam," he commands, his voice a low growl that sends shivers cascading down my spine. "Let me feel you."

His words are my undoing, the coil of tension inside me snapping as I shatter beneath him, my inner walls clenching around his length as ecstasy crashes over me in waves. Colton follows me over the edge with a hoarse shout, his hips stuttering against mine as he spills himself deep inside me, branding me as his own.

We cling to each other in the aftermath, our hearts pounding in sync as we catch our breath. Colton's weight is a welcome anchor, his arms a haven I never knew I needed. He presses soft kisses against my hair, my temple, my lips, each touch a silent promise of something more.

In this moment, wrapped in Colton's embrace, I feel cherished, desired, loved. The insecurities that once plagued me seem to melt away, replaced by a bone-deep certainty that this is where I belong. In his arms, in his bed, in his life.

My cowboy. My husband. My love.

epilogue

. . .

One year later

Colton

THE SUN SETS purple and orange over the hills as I drive the old pickup down the dusty road, one arm resting out the window. The wind whips through my hair and a rare smile plays at my lips. The bank came through with the loan to keep the ranch going. We ain't rich by any means, but we'll survive. And I aim to celebrate.

I glance over at Sam in the passenger seat, her auburn hair glowing like fire in the fading light. She's gazing out at the landscape, lost in thought but looking more at peace than I've seen her. My heart swells. This woman's stood by me through the worst of times. The least I can do is treat her to a nice evening out, even if it's just burgers and shakes in town.

"Almost there, darlin'," I say, reaching over to squeeze her hand. "Figured we both could use a little break from ranch cooking."

She turns to me and smiles, her green eyes sparkling. "You're spoiling me, Colton Westbrook. What's the special occasion?"

"Just feeling mighty grateful is all. For the ranch. For you." I pull her hand to my lips, pressing a Kiss to her knuckles. "Couldn't have made it through without you, Sam. I hope you know that."

Color rises in her cheeks as she ducks her head. "I haven't done much. You're the one who's worked so hard to keep everything going."

"We're a team, honey. Don't you forget it." I turn into the gravel lot of the diner, switching off the engine. "What do you say we leave the ranch behind for a bit and just enjoy ourselves? Like a real date."

Her smile widens. "I'd like that very much."

I hop out and come around to open her door, offering my hand to help her down. She takes it and slides out gracefully. I don't let go as we head inside, enjoying the connection.

Over burgers and fries, we talk and laugh more than we have in ages. The jukebox plays old country tunes and the neon signs paint her skin in a rosy glow. Looking at her, all I can think is how lucky I am. How much I want her by my side, always.

An idea starts forming. Something I shoulda done long ago. When the last fry is gone, I pay the check and lead her back outside into the cool evening air.

"Let's take a little walk," I suggest, nodding toward the park across the street. Twinkling lights are strung through the trees there, making it look downright magical.

She agrees readily, leaning into my side as we meander down the paved path. I'm keenly aware of her soft curves pressed close and take deep breaths of her rose-scented hair.

"Sure is a pretty night," she remarks. "I'm glad you brought me here. It's nice to get away for a bit."

"Well, it ain't over yet." I steer her to a bench beneath a willow tree and gently ease her down to sit. "There's something I need to ask you, Sam."

Her brow furrows in confusion as I crouch

down in front of her. "Colton? What are you doing?"

"Something I should've done properly the first time." Her eyes go wide.

"Sam, I ain't a man of many words. But I do know my life wouldn't be worth much without you in it. You're my partner, my helpmate, and my best friend. Marrying you was the smartest thing I've ever done. But I want you to know, it's more than just an arrangement to me now.

"I love you, darlin'. With everything I got. And I'm asking if you'll be my wife. For real this time. Because you want to. Not because you need to."

Now, I know I ain't got a ring, but I'll let you pick out whatever one you want from the jeweler up the street."

Tears glisten in her eyes as she presses a hand to her mouth. "Oh, Colton..."

"Is that a yes?" I prompt hopefully.

"Yes!" She launches herself into my arms, nearly knocking me back on my rear. "Yes, of course I'll marry you. I love you too!"

Joy like I've never known floods through me. I crush her to my chest, burying my face in her neck. "I'm gonna do everything I can to make you happy, sweetheart. I swear it."

"You already do," she whispers. "You already do."

We hold each other there under the lights, breathing each other in, and then I take her straight to the jewelry store. She picks out a ring. Nothing too flashy—just something simple and elegant.

Like her.

When I pull back to slip the ring onto her finger, I swear my hands are shaking. But it slides on true.

A perfect fit. Just like her in my life.

"What do you say we make this official?" I ask. "Not a big affair, but maybe your friend from town could come along with my brother as witnesses."

I was happy when Sam struck up a friendship with the girl who works at the diner. She needed some female companionship.

She winds her arms around my neck and nods happily. "I think that sounds wonderful. You, me, a simple ceremony. It's all I need."

"Me too, darlin'. Me too."

The very next day, I stand across from her in the town's little whitewashed chapel as her friend Ellen and my brother Pete take their seats. Sam's a vision in an ivory sundress, daisies woven into her fiery waves.

My hands swallow hers as the preacher leads us in our vows. But I'm not nervous anymore. Just deep-in-the-bones certain that this is right. That she's mine and I'm hers.

The words "husband and wife" are music to my ears. She smiles up at me with tears on her lashes. I don't wait for an invitation to kiss my bride.

I may not have much. But I have her. And that's everything I need.

***

After a few congratulatory hugs, we bid our guests goodbye and head back to the ranch. A life of hot, sweaty chores threatens to loom over us, but with Sam by my side, I know we can handle it.

"You up for some celebrating?" I ask, waggling my eyebrows as I grab two cold beers from the pantry.

"Celebrating, huh?" she says with a playful lilt in her voice. "What did you have in mind, cowboy?"

"Oh, I've got a few ideas."

I lead her to the front porch, our boots thudding in unison on the creaky steps. It's dusk now, the sky a watercolor masterpiece of pinks, purples, and oranges. Crickets chirp their congratulations, and an owl hooting in the distance adds to the ambiance.

I clear my throat, suddenly tongue-tied. Sam's

beauty in the soft, golden light takes my breath away.

"Colton?" she prompts, brows knit together in confusion.

I squeeze her hand, willing myself to find the right words. "Samantha Westbrook...I...love you. More than I ever thought possible. Fuck, honey, you get more beautiful to me every day. Keep going this way and you're going to kill me."

My cock is already hard, and I grab her hand and place it on it. "See what you do to me, wife?"

She grins, a smile of satisfaction on her face. "Well, what are you going to do about it, cowboy?"

I growl as I pull her into my arms.

"I'm going to fuck a baby into your belly like a man's supposed to do, that's what."

I capture her startled gasp with my mouth, my cock already leaking at the thought of filling her up with my seed and impregnating her.

Breeding her.

Sam melts against me, her soft curves molding to my hard planes. I back her up against the porch railing, my hands roaming greedily over her body. She mewls into my mouth as I palm her full breasts through the thin sundress fabric.

"Colton," she pants as I trail open-mouthed

kisses down the elegant column of her throat. "I need you."

A possessive thrill shoots through me at her words. I sweep her up into my arms and carry her over the threshold, just like a proper husband should. She clings to my neck, nuzzling under my jaw and sending sparks skittering across my skin.

In our bedroom, I set her on her feet only to slowly peel the dress from her body. It pools at her ankles and she steps out of it, clad only in white lace. My mouth goes dry at the sight.

"God almighty, you're a vision," I rasp, drinking in the dips and swells of her figure, the creamy expanses of skin, the dark auburn curls at the apex of her thighs.

"I'm all yours," she whispers, green eyes dark with desire. "Now and always."

I strip off my own clothes in record time, desperate to feel her skin on mine. When I gather her in my arms again, the slide of her silken flesh against my rougher body is pure bliss. I walk us to the bed and lay her down gently, following to cover her body with my own.

"I love you, Samantha," I murmur against her lips. "I'm going to show you just how much."

I worship every inch of her with hands and mouth, cataloging each breathy sigh and wanton moan. She arches beneath me, flushed and panting, as I suckle at her pert nipples until they're glistening peaks.

"Please, Colton," she begs, writhing restlessly. "I need you."

"I've got you, darlin'." I settle between her parted thighs, the head of my cock nudging insistently at her entrance. "Gonna fill this sweet pussy up until you're dripping with my seed. Gonna make you swell with my child."

She cries out, blunt nails digging into my shoulders as I surge forward, sheathing myself to the hilt in her tight, wet heat. We both groan at the exquisite sensation. I start to move, rolling my hips in a primal rhythm, making sure to hit that spot I know she loves.

She meets me thrust for thrust, undulating beneath me and gasping my name like a prayer. Our bodies move in perfect synchronization, skin slick with sweat, the air heavy with the scent of sex.

"That's it, honey," I growl, angling my hips to hit that secret spot inside her that makes her keen. "Milk my cock. Take every last drop. Wanna fill this belly up with my baby."

A filthy groan rips from my throat at the thought. Sam's pussy clenches around me, her back bowing off the bed. "Yes, Colton! Give me your baby. I want it so bad!"

Her words nearly undo me. A few more frenzied thrusts and I'm emptying myself deep inside her, jet after jet of my hot seed flooding her womb. "Fuck, Samantha. Breeding this sweet cunt. Gonna look so good all round with my child."

She sobs my name as her own release crashes over her, her silken walls milking me for everything I've got. Wave after wave of pleasure rocks through us both as we cling to each other, lost in the throes of passion.

When the tremors finally subside, I gather her close, tucking her head under my chin. Our racing hearts gradually slow, breaths evening out. I press a tender kiss to her damp forehead.

"I love you, Sam. More than anything."

"I love you too, Colton. So much." Her voice is soft with drowsy contentment.

We lay there in the moonlight filtering through the curtains, her tracing idle patterns on my sweat-cooled chest while I run my fingers through her tangled hair. The future stretches out before us, full of promise. Hard work and struggle, no doubt. But also love and partnership. Building a family together on this land that's in my blood.

With Sam in my arms and the ranch pulling

through, I feel a deep sense of peace settle in my bones. A rightness. Come what may, we'll weather it. Together.

I place my palm reverently over her belly, wondering if my seed has already taken root. The thought fills me with a fierce joy and protectiveness.

"Sweet dreams, honey," I whisper as her eyes flutter closed and her breathing deepens. "Tomorrow's a new day."

As I let sleep claim me, I thank the stars above for bringing this woman into my life and into my heart.

My perfect bride.

Want a free book from Emma Bray? Go to www.authoremmabray.com.

Keep reading for an excerpt from Unmasking the Billionaire.

Eve

"I can't believe I let you talk me into this!" I practically have to yell over the music to be heard by Jenny, my best friend since childhood.

Jenny just smiles her dazzling, millionaire-dollar, rich girl smile at me from behind her sparkling, Swarovski-crystal mask.

We're at some sort of masquerade ball for New York's elite. It's the Halloween party of the season and surprisingly not as stuffy as I'd expected it to be.

Honestly, it's kind of cool with the dim lighting, high-end decorations, elaborate costumes, and all the masked faces on parade, but still.

This isn't my element.

"Oh, come on, Eve! This is fun! You need to lighten up and live a little for once!"

That's easy for her to say. She's a trust fund baby without a care in the world. Her mommy and daddy pay for everything, from her expensive haircut to the designer shoes on her feet. She doesn't have to worry about anything.

Not that I begrudge my bestie anything. I'm glad she hasn't had the same struggles in life I've had. It's how she's able to have that beautiful, happy glow about her.

She doesn't know the worry that I do of how she's going to pay next month's rent or how she's going to juggle the electric bill so that the power doesn't get cut off.

And while she's offered to pay my bills before or let me move in with her, I have way too much pride to accept her offers.

I've been making it on my own since I turned eighteen and aged out of the group home, and I'm not about to start accepting charity now that I'm twenty.

"Your birthday only comes around once a year!" she reminds me, flinging an arm around my shoulder familiarly. "It's time to turn up and party!" She pronounces "party" like "par-tay," and I can't help the smile that ghosts across my lips at her giddiness.

Jenny is a blonde bombshell. Model thin, tan, and tall, she's all bubbly and light whereas I almost look like a goth chick with my midnight black hair, pale complexion, and short stature. And although Jenny's slender, she has a little bit of curves in all the right places.

Me? Nothing. I'm so thin my breasts and ass are laughable at best, and it's not because I don't eat because trust me. I've gone hungry before, and you'll never see me turn down a meal or feign a weak appetite. I can put it away like a football player, and I'm not even the least bit ashamed of it.

At barely five foot, though, I'm teeny tiny and still look like a pre-teen—no matter how much I eat.

My best friend and I are total opposites. She's outgoing whereas I'm quieter. I'm not exactly shy, but I don't have a desire to be the life of the party either. She's like the light, and I'm the dark. Seriously, I was born on All Hallow's Eve, and she was born on Jesus' birthday, a perfect little Christmas baby.

"Come on," Jenny grabs my hand and starts dragging me along with her, "let's go find some hot guys."

I roll my eyes. That's another difference between us. Jenny is boy crazy, and I couldn't care less about the opposite sex. I'm not a lesbian or anything, but I just don't have any experience with men.

Survival has kept me from getting into any serious relationships. The most I've ever done is let a few boyfriends in high school kiss me, and I wasn't impressed with those slobbery attempts, so I've never been tempted to even try anything more.

So, yeah, I'm a twenty-year-old virgin. Pathetic, right?

Jenny drags me by a table filled with Halloween-themed cookies, cakes, and other confections, and my mouth begins to water.

I pull back on her hand to try to stay her. "Let's get some refreshments instead!" I yell to her over the pumping music.

She looks over her shoulder at me and rolls her eyes. "I swear, Eve, you're always freaking hungry. I don't know where you put it all."

I smirk at the obvious envy in her tone. Jenny is the stereotypical gym bunny, counting every calorie she eats to maintain her perfect physique.

"Don't hate," I grin at her smugly before reaching out to grab a miniature black cupcake covered with purple frosting.

I barely have time to pop the bite-sized confection in my mouth before Jenny is yanking on my hand again, pulling me through the crowd.

"Jenny, slow down!" I hiss at her, afraid I'm going to break my neck in these five-inch heels she insisted I wear tonight to make me not look like so much of a smurf. Her words—not mine. Plus, she claims they're just the perfect addition to the lacy black dress she dressed me up in.

I swear sometimes I think Jenny is my friend just because she wants a real-life doll to play dress up with. There's no greater joy for her than dressing me up in fancy clothes, doing my hair and makeup, and dragging me to shit like this with her.

And I go along with it because I love my best friend and want to make her happy.

Her eyes are scanning through all the masculine choices, and then she suddenly stops dead in her tracks.

"Oh. My. God." she breaths out.

"What?" my brows furrow at her melodramatic reaction.

"Check out Mr. Big and Scary," she breathes, and my eyes follow her line of sight and widen when they meet the object of her gaze.

A huge man in a black mask stands in a corner looking surly and brooding, towering over the other guests. The mask covers most of his face except his mouth. Think of the Don Juan mask Gerard Butler wore in *The Point of No Return* scene in that film adaptation of *The Phantom of the Opera*. That's what his mask reminds me of.

His hair is dark brown. It's stylishly disheveled, like it's windblown and wild without looking messy. When he tilts his tumbler up and takes a sip of some liquid that's probably brandy or cognac or something else equally expensive, I watch his suit rustle as his muscles bunch with his movements like it's all the fabric can do to contain the beast within.

I don't know who the hell the guy is or what he

does, but he exudes power and wealth. He's not wearing a costume like the other partygoers. No, he's wearing what I already know is a custom-tailored suit.

I don't need to be able to see all his features to see that he's gorgeous and dark and dangerous-looking. I've never seen a more perfect specimen of male masculinity, and my heart speeds up as my breath catches in my throat.

I've never reacted to a man this way before, and Jenny notices it if the sly, mischievous grin she gives me is any indication.

"I dare you to go over there and kiss him," she elbows me.

I laugh and push her back. "You're crazy! I'm not going to do that! I don't even know the guy."

"Exactly!" Jenny's eyes are excited. "You don't know him…" her voice sing-songs, "he's super smexy."

I roll my eyes. Only Jenny would make "smexy" a word in conversation.

Jenny ignores me and goes on, "You're twenty years old today, and you've never had a decent kiss."

I glare at her, suddenly wishing I hadn't told her all the embarrassing details of my failed boyfriends.

Again she ignores me and keeps ticking off reasons I should follow her insane suggestion. "It's dark in here, and you'll never have to see him again. You can simply go lay one on the hot stranger and have a great memory for your birthday, and then we'll go eat cake and dance and party and everything will be perfect! You have nothing to lose and everything to gain!" she says happily.

I stare at her like she's sprouted another head.

Jenny is seriously out of her mind sometimes.

I'm laughing and shaking my head 'no' at her when she narrows her eyes and adds, "Plus, I'll give you a thousand dollars if you do it."

My laugh dies off as I nearly choke. "Whoa, wait. What?" I shake my head at her. "You can't be serious, right?"

Jenny's not laughing, though. She's looking at me challengingly with that I-want-to-get-you-in-trouble look that only a best friend can have.

"Dead serious. I'll give you a thousand bucks to walk over there and kiss that guy." She nods her head in his direction before that evil twinkle enters her eyes again. "And not just a quick peck on the lips. A real kiss. Like with some tongue."

I glance back over at Mr. Smexy. Jesus, did I just refer to him as Mr. Smexy in my head? I obviously need new friends. Jenny is rubbing off on me too much.

The man might be good-looking, but he's terrifying too. God, he could crush me with one hand.

And what the fuck will he think when some random girl comes up and kisses him out of the blue?

He'll probably have me arrested.

I'll embarrass the hell out of myself.

God, am I really considering this?

But, fuck, a thousand dollars? That'd give me a huge boost on paying my bills.

I look back over at Jenny. She's grinning at me impishly. She knows my struggle, and I think she halfway expects me to chicken out and not do it.

And that is what cements my decision.

I cross my arms and tell Jenny, "I want it in cash."

I see the surprise skitter across Jenny's face before she raises one delicate eyebrow and smiles like the Cheshire Cat, the glee practically oozing off her as she claps her hands together and laughs, "You got it, babe."

Before I lose my nerve, I take a deep breath, square my shoulders, and begin making my way over to the corner where Mr. Smexy skulks like some kind of standoffish canine.

I can almost feel Jenny's eyes boring a hole into my back, taking in the whole scene.

A thousand dollars. A thousand dollars, I chant in my head with each step I take.

As I get closer to him, he starts to notice my approach.

His head tips up, and his eyes laser in on me. The lighting is so dim where he's standing, it's hard to make out his features, but his eyes are golden and almost seem to glow like he's a vampire or wolf or something.

I swallow nervously and try to calm my racing heart.

A thousand dollars. A thousand dollars.

I just hope he doesn't bite me.

———

Lucian

My eyes are trained on a tiny form making its way in my direction, and they narrow as it gets closer.

It's dark in here, and lights flash out on the dance floor, but I've sequestered myself in this corner for a reason.

I don't want to be bothered.

In fact, the only reason I'm here is to meet with a business associate, and the fucker is late.

I'd much rather be back at my mansion. Alone. Secluded. The way I like to be.

I have no use for people beyond employing them.

Social settings aren't my scene and for good reason. The only reason I agreed to see my associate here is because he's only going to be in town for one night, and this is where he's going to be.

For some God forsaken reason.

And it's a masquerade-themed Halloween ball, so I can cover my scarred face. It's not that I particularly give a fuck what people think about it. I know that I'm still considered handsome, that maybe the cut that spans right side of my visage simply gives me that allure of danger that some women find so enticing.

But it's the questions I can't stand. The curiosity. The goddamned nosiness.

People don't know me. Nobody seeks me out. My demeanor is just menacing enough to off-put any curious eyes that glance my way.

So why in the hell does this little slip of a thing seem to be walking my way?

My eyes take in her long, dark tresses that flow

down to her impossibly tiny waist. Milky white skin that almost seems to glow in the darkness.

Fuck, she's covered in lace. Her dress must be corseted if the way the two little globes of her breasts are pushed up is any indication. They're not large by any means, but just the sight of that little bit of modest cleavage has my blood roaring in my veins.

How long has it been since I've been with a woman? Since before the incident five years ago at least. I know I have enough money that I can still have plenty of women on my arm if I want.

That's not what I want, though. Shallow companions, fake smiles.

Since I can't have a connection, something real, I settle for nothing.

My hands work just fine.

But Christ Almighty, seeing a female approaching me after all this time has every nerve in my body pulled taut. I'm on edge and feel like I could blow at any moment.

My eyes drag back up her form to her head, most of which is covered with an elaborate peacock mask.

I can't make out her features through the dim lighting and all the ostentatious feathers that cover her face, but I see a flash of midnight blue before she's suddenly standing right in front of me. Her body isn't touching mine, but she's so close that I can feel her heat through our clothes, smell her scent. Violets and vanilla and something I can't identify.

Her head barely reaches my chest, and before I can ask her what she's doing, who she is, hell, anything, I hear her take a deep breath, and then she clumsily grabs my face and pulls it down to hers, pressing her lips firmly, if somewhat nervously, against mine.

I'm so stunned I don't react at first. But then my mind and body registers the feel of her tiny lips on mine. They're pressing softly against them, and then she takes my bottom lip in between her lips in an innocent, single-lip kiss. It's unpracticed, but god there's something so fucking hot about it, I feel a drop of precum bead the tip of my suddenly hard cock.

Hunger, hot and immediate, roars in my chest and bleeds through my veins.

I don't think. I just react, my hand reaching out to fist in her hair as I angle her head up to mine, deepening the kiss.

I suck on her bottom lip before my tongue forces her mouth to part, and she does so with a gasp of surprise.

I lick inside her mouth and taste her. Fucking hell, she tastes so goddamned sweet. Like pure sugar.

She whimpers, and that sound only spurs me on. I growl and mate my tongue with hers, desperate for more. More of her mouth. More of her.

I don't know who the fuck she is, but I know I'm not just turned into an animal because of five years of abstinence.

This is something more. Something primal. Like a wolf imprinting on its mate.

She tastes so fucking *right*. That might be a cliche, but fuck if I can help what I'm thinking and feeling.

Never, I mean, *never*, has a mere kiss affected me this way.

Just as I manage to set my glass of cognac down on a nearby table and am getting ready to pull her flush against my body, maybe throw her over my shoulder and stomp out of here caveman style and take her back to my lair and make her mine, she pulls away harshly, her little hands pressing hard against my chest.

We're both panting. I watch her little chest moving up and down as she gasps for breath. Her lips are ruby red and puffy and swollen from our kiss. I'm dying to see her eyes again, to demand who she is, where she came from, why the hell she planted her little lips on mine, but I never get a chance to ask any of that because she never looks back up at me.

Quick as a flash, she turns and runs away from me.

Panic explodes in my chest when I see her flying through the crowd.

Just as I start to take off after her, Adrian shows up and claps a heavy hand on my shoulder.

"Lucian, my man!" he greets me jovially.

I glance over at him distractedly, irritated that he took my attention off my little raven.

By the time I look back into the crowd, she's nowhere to be found. Rage and loss bubble up inside me to create a nauseating cocktail of emotions.

And I want to fucking murder someone.